JULIANA BUTTERFLY

Deborah Ribar Tibbs

Illustrated by: John Riggle

A great big thank you to: My wonderful husband, Larry Tibbs; Mary Martin—the greatest mom in the world; Louis, Jamie, Michael and Leah Ribar (for being my everything!); William, Kaleb, Emberlynn, Alexandra and Chad Shearer; Rick Hansberry; Michael Eshleman; John Riggle; and Demi Stevens. Thank you for believing in me and helping me make this dream come true.

ISBN 13: 978-1523275205

ISBN 10: 1523275200

To my Juliana Butterfly

May you always find

your way home.

"Don't fly so far away, Juliana Butterfly,"
Mother Butterfly said.
"You are going too fast.
You are getting too far ahead!"

"The world is so big,
you might lose your way.
I might not be able to find you
at the end of the day."

"But I want to see the world!"
Juliana Butterfly cried.
"It's all so beautiful
and the sky so vast and wide!"

"I want to see all there is to see...
to explore every land,
to fly across the ocean and
make butterfly angels in the sand."

"I'll play hide & seek amongst the trees.
That sounds like so much fun.
I'll land in the leafy treetops
and rest beneath the golden sun."

"I'll play tag in the park
with the bright yellow bees.
I'll sail with the eagles and
catch a ride on the summer breeze."

So she spread her colorful wings
and into the big blue sky she flew.
Despite Mother Butterfly's warning
she set off to find something new.

She saw snow in the mountaintops
and colorful fish in the sea.
She played tag in the park
with the bright yellow bees.

She counted lovely flowers
that decorated the land.
She flew across the ocean and
made butterfly angels in the sand.

Soon the daylight began to dim.
Juliana Butterfly had to find her way home.
But she didn't know where she was
or which way she had come.

Aimlessly she flew,
winding through towering trees.
A strong wind blew through,
tangling her in the summer breeze.

The wind swept her up.
She tumbled through the air.
She finally broke free,
but had no idea where!

Her tiny wings tired,
her courage began to fade.
"I should've stayed closer to home.
What a big mistake I made!"

"I should've listened to Mother Butterfly.
She *always* knows what's right.
I could be home right now,
If I hadn't put up such a fight."

"I wish Mother Butterfly was *here*," Juliana Butterfly said.
"She'd take me safely home, and tuck me into bed."

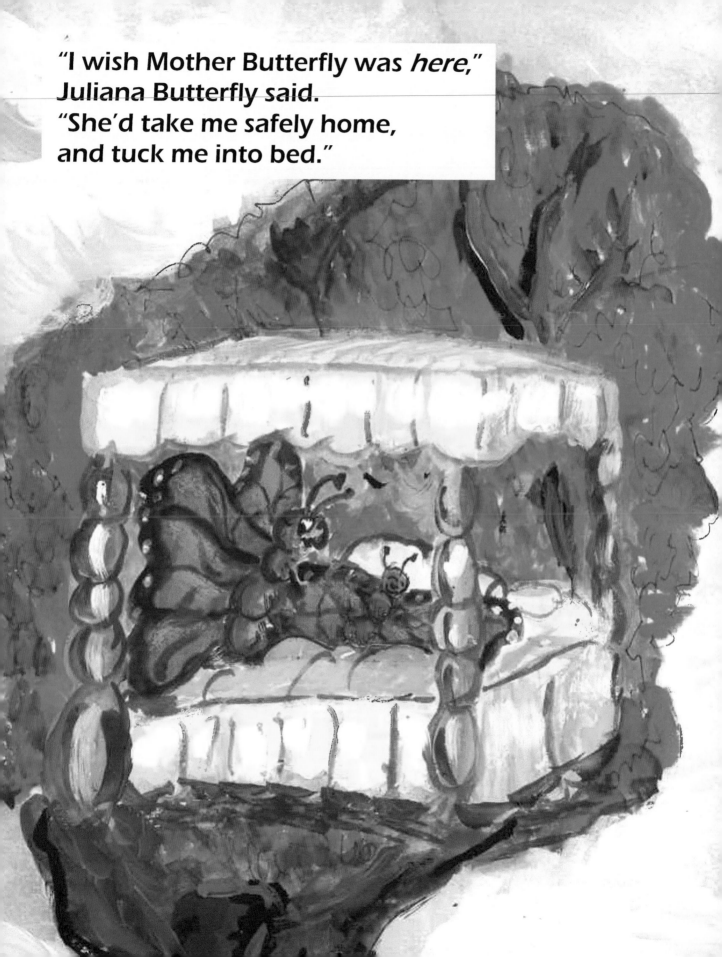

Juliana Butterfly was tired and lonely
and soon began to cry.
"Mother Butterfly!" she yelled.
"Tell me which way to fly!"

"Look this way,"
she heard a familiar voice say.
"If you listen to me now,
I'll help you find your way."

"Mother Butterfly!" Juliana Butterfly sobbed.
"How did you know I was here?
I thought I was lost forever!" she cried
as Mother Butterfly wiped away her tears.

"You never have to worry.
You never have to fear.
Because you are my Juliana Butterfly,
I will *always* keep you near."

Deborah Ribar Tibbs has the honor of being the mother to four amazing children, Louis, Jamie, Michael and Leah Ribar. Her daughter Jamie has blessed her with five wonderful grandchildren. Juliana is her first granddaughter. Deborah Ribar Tibbs works as a legal assistant at CGA Law Firm and lives in York, PA, with her brand new husband Larry "Lar-Bear" Tibbs.